KING
BABY

KATE BEATON

WALKER BOOKS
AND SUBSIDIARIES
LONDON • BOSTON • SYDNEY • AUCKLAND

First published in Great Britain 2016 by Walker Books Ltd
87 Vauxhall Walk, London SE11 5HJ

2 4 6 8 10 9 7 5 3 1

© 2016 Kate Beaton

The right of Kate Beaton to be identified as the author and illustrator of this work
has been asserted by her in accordance with the Copyright,
Designs and Patents Act 1988

First published in the United States 2016 by Arthur A. Levine Books, an imprint of Scholastic Inc.
British publication rights arranged with Abner Stein Ltd.

This book has been typeset in Trocchi Regular

Printed in China

British Library Cataloguing in Publication Data:
a catalogue record for this book is available from the British Library

ISBN 978-1-4063-7175-8

wwww.walker.co.uk

For Malcolm

I am King Baby!

Yes, come!
You have been waiting for me.

I will give you many blessings,
for King Baby is generous.

You will have smiles and laughs and kisses.

You will have wiggles
and gurgles and coos!

But your king also has many demands!

FEED ME!

BURP ME!

CHANGE ME!

BOUNCE ME!

CARRY ME!

It is good to be the king.

Now. Bring me the thing.

Not this thing! The other thing!
Bring me the other thing!

These subjects are fools!

King Baby must do
something bold and new.

King Baby
will get the thing
HIMSELF!

)) PLOP

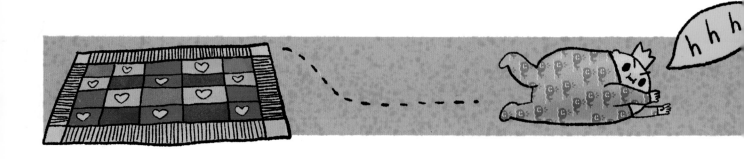

hhh

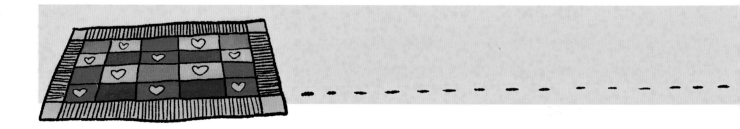

Yes. King Baby can do it.

King Baby will get the thing.

Nothing will stop King Baby!

Crawling, of course!
But why stop at crawling?

King Baby will walk.
And talk. And MORE!

His future is glory! For King Baby i

…o longer a baby. He shall become…

A big boy.

But what of these poor subjects?

Who are they, without a king?

And who will lead them, if not I?

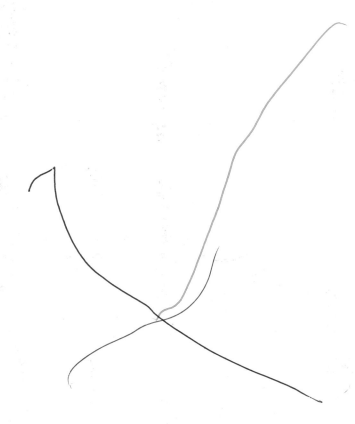

I am Queen Baby.

Kate Beaton is the author of *The Princess and the Pony*, as well as the #1 New York Times bestselling comics collections *Hark! A Vagrant* and *Step Aside, Pops*. She lives in Nova Scotia, Canada and is Aunt Katie to little Malcolm, the King Baby of her heart. Find her online at www.beatontown.com and on Twitter as @beatonna.

Look out for:

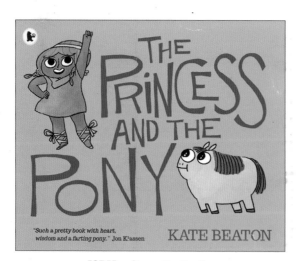

ISBN 978-1-4063-6538-2

"Such a pretty book with heart, wisdom and a farting pony"
Jon Klassen

"Hits the picture book jackpot of making children and adults laugh"
Bookseller

"Everything about this book should be a sure-fire winner"
Guardian

Available from all good booksellers

www.walker.co.uk